To Marloes and Kasper

and may Susan be thanked

Production and copyright © 1992 Rainbow Grafics International—
Baronian Books SC, Brussels, Belgium.
English translation text copyright © 1993 by Lothrop, Lee & Shepard Books.
All rights reserved. No part of this book may be reproduced or utilized in any
form or by any means, electronic or mechanical, including photocopying and
recording, or by any information storage and retrieval system, without permis-
sion in writing from the Publisher. Inquiries should be addressed to Lothrop, Lee
& Shepard Books, a division of William Morrow & Company, Inc., 1350 Avenue
of the Americas, New York, New York 10019. Printed in Belgium. Printed in EEC.

First Edition   1   2   3   4   5   6   7   8   9   10

Library of Congress Cataloging in Publication data was not available in time for
publication of this book, but can be obtained from the Library of Congress.
ISBN 0-688-12381-3   Library of Congress Catalog Card Number: 92-54428

WHAT KOUKA KNOWS

BY TRUUS

LOTHROP, LEE & SHEPARD BOOKS

NEW YORK

Kouka has a problem.
If he goes to Daniel's tea party...

he won't have time to decorate Dolly.

If he plays ball with Bill...

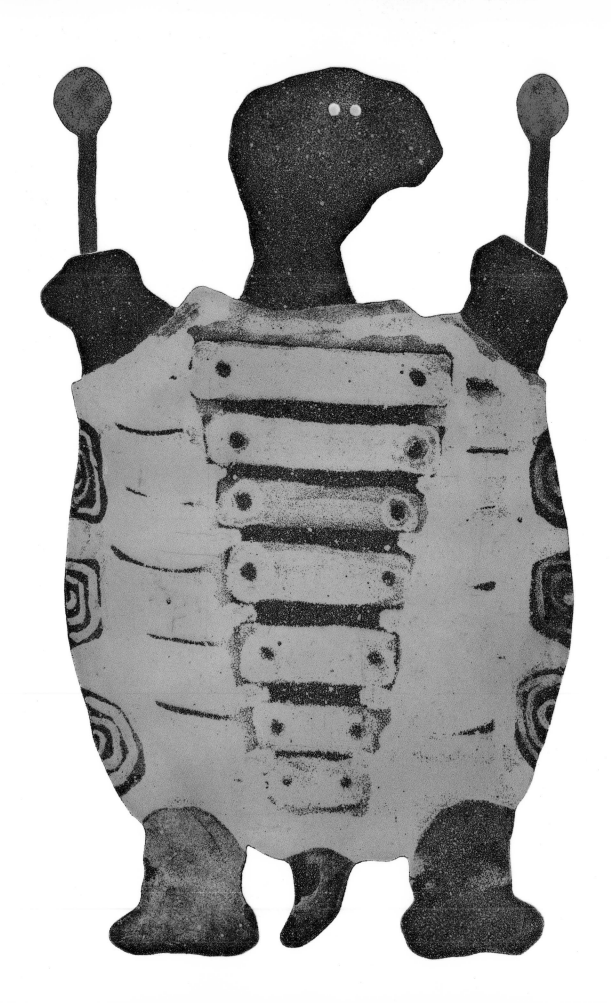

he'll never fit in Margaret's music lesson.

If he helps Charles learn to fly...

how will he have time
for hide-and-seek with Fred?

he will miss Harriet's haircut.

If he high jumps with Henrietta...

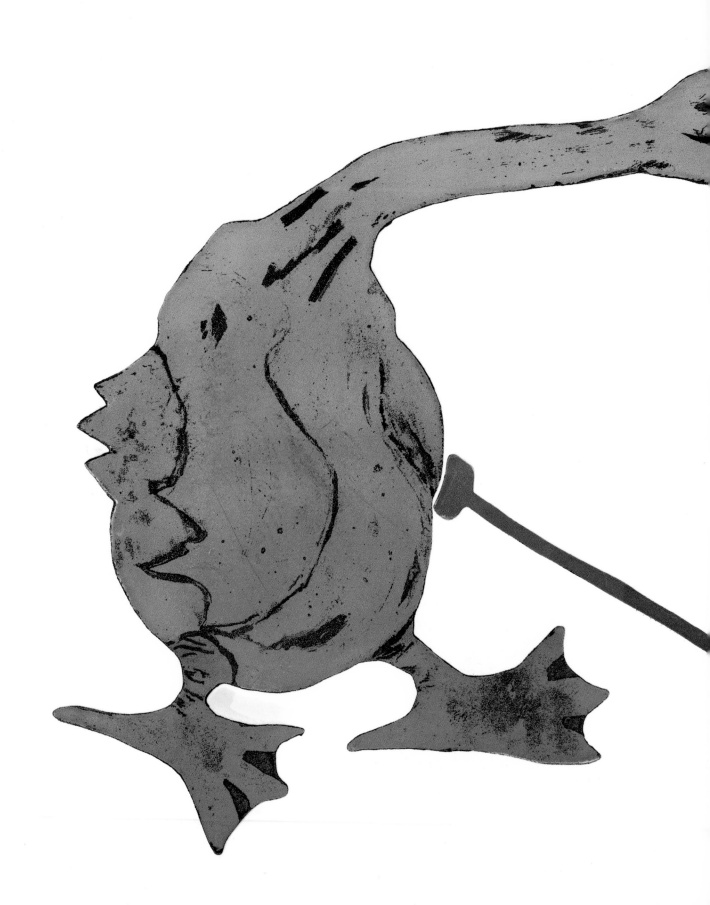

If he takes a ride with Gertrude...

he'll have no time left for Barnaby's bath.
It's a big problem...

but Kouka knows a way
to play with *all* his friends!

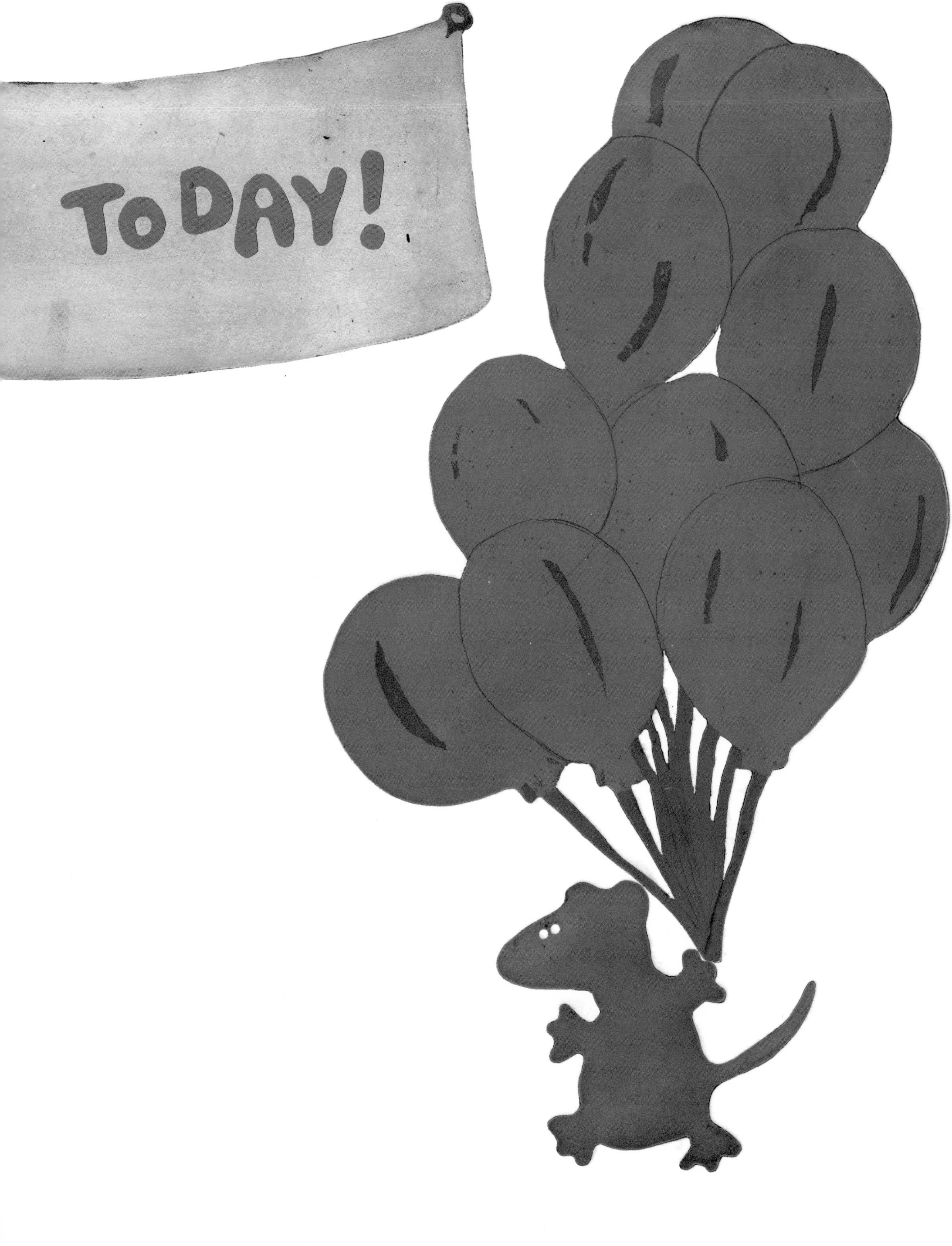
TODAY!